Tiny Tatty Teddy's
Christmas

Autumn
Publishing

Autumn
Publishing

Published in 2016
by Autumn Publishing
Cottage Farm
Sywell
NN6 0BJ
www.igloobooks.com

Designed by Elitsa Veshkova
Edited by Gemma Rose

REX001 0716
2 4 6 8 10 9 7 5 3 1
ISBN 978-1-78557-478-8

Produced under license for

carte blanche

Printed and manufactured in China

This Autumn book belongs to:

....

It's Christmas Eve and Tiny Tatty Teddy is busy getting ready for Christmas Day.

There is so much to do!

First of all, Tiny decorates the Christmas tree with lots of pretty decorations.

There are red baubles, sparkly tinsel and a star for the top of the tree.

Next, Tiny gets sheets of shiny wrapping paper and wraps lots of presents for friends and family.

The gifts are finished neatly with a pretty ribbon.

What is Tiny doing now?
He is hanging up the stockings ready for
Father Christmas to fill with presents.

Look! Tiny has found an enormous stocking.

Father Christmas will have to put lots of presents in this one!

Tiny sits down with a pen and paper
to begin writing to Father Christmas.

There are lots of toys he would like.

Tiny wishes for a little blue and green rocket to send shooting into space.

Whoosh! Time for take off!

Or a red toy car to push around the garden.
Toot, toot! Vroom, vroom! Coming through!

How about a big stripy ball to bounce?
Boing, boing, boing.

Boing!
Boing!
Boing!

Tiny can't wait to see what presents
Father Christmas will bring.

Suddenly, he notices it is snowing.
Tiny feels the soft, white flakes

falling

from

the

sky.

Crunch, crunch, crunch go the
little bear's feet on the snow.
It's so much fun to play outside.

Tiny decides to take handfuls of snow and roll them into balls.

Brr! The snow makes his hands tingle.

What has Tiny made? It's a snowman.
He adds a carrot for a nose, stones
for eyes and a red woolly hat.

Next, Tiny gets out a little red sledge and goes whizzing around the garden.

Weeeeeeee

Weeee, hold on tight! The snow is so magical.

Back inside, he warms up and looks out of the window waiting for Father Christmas. He isn't here yet, Tiny!

Father Christmas and his reindeer won't come until you're fast asleep.

Let's get ready for bed.

Tiny settles down to read a
good Christmas story.

A Magical Christmas

Father Christmas

Letter To Santa

A Snowy Night

Which one is he going to choose?

After a long day of getting ready for Christmas, Tiny is tired and falls sound asleep.

shhh!

Goodnight, Tiny.

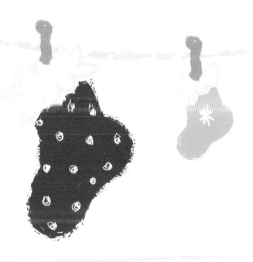

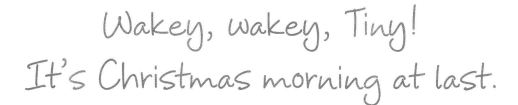
Wakey, wakey, Tiny!
It's Christmas morning at last.

Wakey!
Wakey!

Excitedly, he goes
to see if Father
Christmas has
been to visit.

He has! Look at all the presents.
Tiny loves his toy reindeer the most.
He has been a very lucky bear.

Merry Christmas, Tiny Tatty Teddy!